MW01091813

For Frank, Meg, and Chris—who shared with me a wish upon a star.

——KMB

For all the Milos out there!

——PD

Published by Yeehoo Press
721 W Whittier Blvd, Suite O, La Habra, CA 90631
www.yeehoopress.com

The illustrations for this book were created in photoshop.
This book was designed by Shen Yao.

Library of Congress Control Number: 2021930155
ISBN: 978-1-953458-04-9
Printed in China First Edition
1 2 3 4 5 6 7 8 9 10

Milo's Moonlight Mission

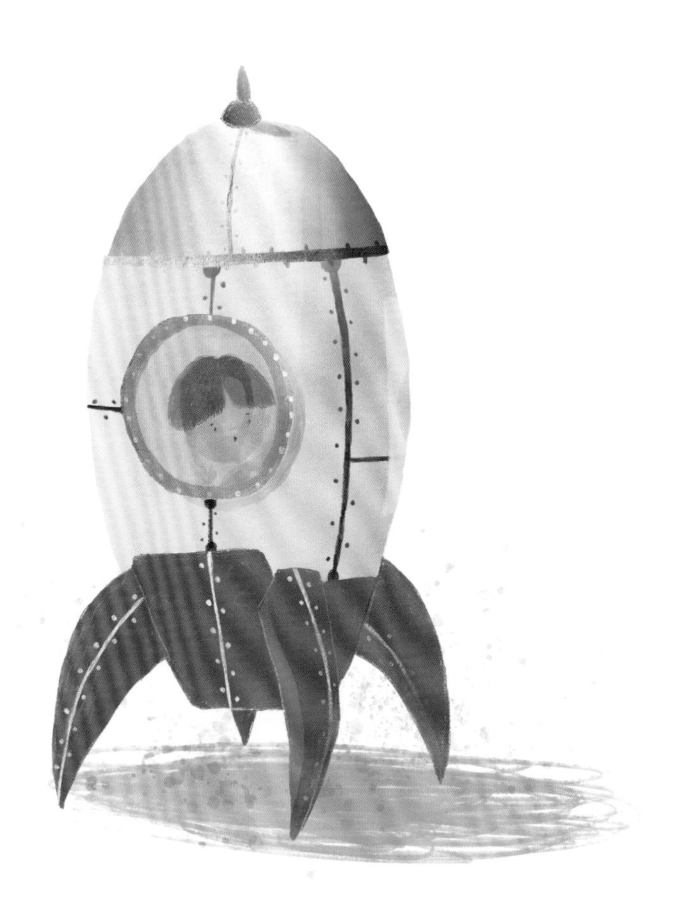

Written by Kathleen M. Blasi
Illustrated by Petronela Dostalova

YEEHOO PRESS

Take offs. Blast offs.

For Milo and his crew, the sky is the limit.

One day, Milo's Second-in-Command
was late for duty.

He found her in her office. “Are you ready for launch?” he asked.

Second-in-Command glanced at the clock. “Sorry, Captain, but I need to finish my work first.”

Like a good captain, Milo offered to help.

Together, they pondered.
He painted. She wrote.
Making stories takes time.
A long time.

The sun stretched shadows across the yard.

“We still have time to get back before dark, Mom,” Milo suggested.

“Maybe,” said Mom. “But soon, the crew here will be hungry.”

Milo sighed, then added, “I‘ll help!”

Together, they mixed.

He stirred. She chopped.

Cooking takes time. A long time.

Milo peered outside.
His hope for a space mission
faded with the setting sun.

Supper chatter. Cleanup clatter. The hum of TV news.

‘And now for tonight’s
orecast!” the announcer said.

Milo turned.

‘Rise before sunrise, if you want
o witness the spectacular Leonid
Meteor Storm!”

"Leonid Meteor Storm," Milo echoed. "The most stunning in decades!"

Mom paused. "Let's call it an early night and get ready for bed."

"Tomorrow," she said, "I have an early meeting with a very important person."

Already? Why?

Mom snuggled beside Milo and read a story. She kissed him goodnight, set his alarm clock, and turned out the light.

Who is Mom going to meet? Milo couldn't sleep. He blinked at the glowing stars on his ceiling.

Pretend stars are good, Milo thought. But real ones are better! Maybe Mom could have time for her important meeting and a meteor storm . . .

With Captain Milo's help!

Milo filled the tea pot, set the counter, and packed sandwiches.

He climbed back into bed.
Will Second-in-Command accept this new mission?
He wished on a dimming ceiling star, then drifted to sleep.

Milo bolted to Mom's room.

He checked her office.

Coffee

Milo found Mom in the kitchen.

"You are a supremely helpful captain," she said, handing Milo his jacket and a blanket. "Thanks to you, we are ready for a meteor mission!"

In the wee hours of morning,
when dark says it's night, Mom and
Milo fixed their eyes to the sky.
Twinkling stars kindled the vast,
black blanket above.

They waited. And then . . .

An invisible paintbrush swept the sky, as one after another, bursts of light sailed through the darkness.
"Like fireworks," whispered Milo.

But . . .

No BANGS . . .

No BOOMS .

No sizzles.

Not a sound.

"Mom," said Milo. "How long can we stay out here, so you're not late for your meeting?"

Mom drew him closer. "That meeting already started, Captain. And I made it just in time."

Star-gazing takes time. A good, long time.
Together, Milo and Mom watched the sky
blink and blaze, then dim with haze,
until the fiery horizon lulled the last star to sleep.

Author's Note

Years ago, my family ventured outside at 4 o'clock, on a chilly November morning, to witness the forecasted Leonid Meteor Storm.

We watched thousands of shooting stars torpedo through the dark sky, with an intensity so rare that meteorologists noted it could be another 100 years before a meteor storm of that magnitude occurs again.

Comets, made of ice and rock, travel around the Sun, leaving behind a trail of debris. When the Earth passes through this trail along its orbit, the debris enters Earth's atmosphere and burns, resulting in meteors, or shooting stars. The brightest meteors display vibrant streaks of color, while fainter ones appear white.

On an average night, fewer than ten meteors occur per hour. Several—even hundreds—of meteors occurring per hour is called a meteor shower. Meteors numbering more than 1,000 per hour are referred to as a meteor storm.

The month of November is known for some of the most remarkable meteor showers and storms. The Leonid Meteor Storm, on which Milo's Moolight Mission is based, occurs when the Earth passes through the debris trail of the comet Tempel-Tuttle. Although the Leonid Meteor Shower occurs each mid-November, the Leonid Meteor Storm occurs about once every 33 years.